T0343116

IB: I'm gonna dedicate the book to you.
BT: Pahahahaha. Why would you do that?
IB: Cos I love you.
BT: Pahahahaha. You don't love me.
IB: I didn't love you before. It just happened this second.
BT: Shut up.
IB: I mean it!
BT: Like you ever do anything straight.
IB: And you do?

I am lying in his arms; he grips one hand around my throat -

BT: I'm gonna fucking marry you.

- so I can't breathe.

BT: I can tell.

That's when I got angry. Started kicking him under the covers.

IB: Don't say things you don't mean. I hate it when people take the piss out of me. It's my worst thing.

He pins me down in a second, puts his hand over my mouth. I struggle to get free, trying to kick him or pull his hair.

BT: Listen, you mad impatient girl, I told you -
IB: *(muffled)* - born for conflict yeah?
BT: Pahahahaha iiiiidiot. Have you seen a documentary called 'Every fucking day of my life'? About a woman whose husband beats her every day for 15 years, and one day her and her son kill him.
IB: And what?
BT: They got 6 and 3 years respectively. What I'm saying is - they'll catch you. Pahahahaha.
IB: I don't think they should lock people up. Or if anything, lock up the victims!
BT: Pahahahaha. You victim you.

To Ben Thomas, with love.

P R O L O G U E

The first time she left home she was 14. Only wearing knickers and a bra and a green felt hat, she walked from Bloomsbury to Peckham looking freaked out enough for no perv to even try it. The next time she left, it was for the summer. She was 15 and lived in an Eden on the roof of a 6th form college, once set aside for basketball. Rooms were marked out along old court lines by barricades of broken furniture - mostly plastic chairs - beneath a giant rusting cage of wire mesh. She left again when she was 16 (lasting a matter of days) and departed to a new address off Queens' Square WC1. In a dark, dark house that had been divided into flats, there was a dark, dark cupboard (used mostly as a bike shed). She poised these revolutionary machines on their back wheels and made a bed beneath them, never thinking that the balancing act might come crashing down on her as she slept. Safe as pyramids. She even had boys over; giggling as footsteps passed above their heads. It lasted four months until a warm spring day prompts a preacher to get on his bomber. He swings open the door and peers inside. She sits up, caught.

"Don't play the blessed middle class martyr. Accept you are a criminal and be prepared to act like one."

That day she spends her last money on a pair of potato guns and roams the streets around the British Museum taking aim at moving targets; the catch of the day being a coachload of disembarking nuns.

These days tho, she is fully postcoded up. Fuck knows what changed.

"Who you calling fucknose?"

You you cunt.

MY SECRCTS
IN THEZAIND
ANDOPENSUY
THEREISNO
LONGTARY
TIMT TOLOSI
THE WORLDIS
YOUNGTUITH
LAUGHTORCANFY
AMONGTH
CBOURSAS
WECHOOSIE!

THERUSHINGM
INUTESPAUSE
ANUNUSEDDAY
BREAKSINTODA
WNANDCHEATS
THETIREDSUN
THCBIRDSARES
INGING.HARL!Q
OMEOUTANDP
LAY!THEREISN
OHURRY!LIFEH
ASJUSTBEGUN!

CONTENTS

✿ ✿

Notes on They

AIT

Hermetic Drift: Lateral surfing through correspondences that often happens when thinking about esoteric ideas.
Connections can be made which are symbolic or poetic and not based necessarily on logic or science.

He winds his way across London, sticking to B roads and backstreets, going ever more southerly, ever more west. He knows the way well, has done this walk a million times, and does not look up until he catches his first glimpse of the Thames. Back to Chiswick. W4. The pavement opens out into wide shelves that drop down in stages to where shady figures populate the banks. The doggers and the dogged. The river is tame this far out. Not like in the east, where churning undercurrents do the job bricks in pockets should; embed debris in silt. He recalls that bloke found under Blackfriars Bridge. GOD'S OWN BANKER SIGNS LAST CHEQUE, the papers read.

City planners force him away from the river and onto a pedestrianised high street for a spell. He walks with his face to the floor, ignoring garish neon shop fronts and gormless mannequins; averting his gaze from everything but the shoppers' shoes whose rhythm he uses to keep pace, so as not to stand out.

You spot him as he disappears up an unlit and unpaved alley running between an Argos and a Waterstones, leaving a trail of black footsteps smudged in the mud in his wake.

If you'll follow him anywhere, go to No. 5

If are glad to see the back of the suicidal loon, go to No. 3

$\overset{\infty}{\text{No.}}$ 1

Chiswick Ait is an island at high tide but when the waters are out, you can just make it walking. If you are planning to stay (and so mind getting wet), use bin bags, one wrapped over each foot and held up to the top of each thigh. There won't be a wet spot deeper than that, though doubling them up might be a good idea.

If your limbs begin dissolving in the water you tread, go to No. 4

If you reach the other side safely, go to No. 6

$\overset{\infty}{\text{No.}}$ 2

Use your hands and feet. When you get to the top, you should be able to hear a hollow ring, what a burp might sound like inside a stomach.

If you lose your balance, go to No. 1

If you feel hungry, go to No. 4

$\overset{\infty}{\text{No.}}$ 3

You saunter into Waterstones and wandering the aisles, spot a small volume tucked between another Hitler biography and a chick-lit, soft-porn slavery romp. *Gentle Art*. There is a note tucked inside. "Please freely distribute this book," it reads. 'Ave it.

Go to any number you choose.

No.$^{\infty}$ 4

Don't worry. You die in most endings anyway.

No.$^{\infty}$ 5

The air smells like diesel. The river looks like a dead snake. But you can't get to it. The way is blocked. Boulders of smashed pebbledash, dazzling with damp; broken concrete with thick steel wiring sticking out.

If you clamber straight across, go to No. 2

If you look to try and find an easier way, go to No.4

No.$^{\infty}$ 6

Once you reach the other side, you find a stone staircase covered with moss. You begin walking up it.

If you crawl up on all fours, go to No. 4.

If you slither up on your belly, go to No. 7

No.$^{\infty}$ 7

The size of Chiswick Ait is deceptive. A dense copse of cedars survives there. Their debris covers the island's floor, and twigs float in the churning water at its edges. Fallen branches hang from the trees, and all the time, more keep falling. Straight as arrows. Or are they* being thrown? You hear laughter. Pahahaha. Where the - and what was that? A stone aimed for your head. And another. You swing yourself up into the low branches of the closest tree, to hide and to get a better look. Up there is a man. Pale and dishevelled. Jacketless and shoeless. You can find him here any day, face turned to the sky, in habitual conversation with the angels.

∞

LET G
LET G
LET G
LET G
LET G
LET G

OD GO
OD GO
OD GO
OD GO
OD GO
OD GO

They* wrestle him roughly out of the Minimart and throw him unceremoniously onto the forecourt. Dropping the money, George lifts his left hand to his face, blind fingers inspecting where rubble is embedded in his chin.

The night-shift have abandoned their tasks and improvised a neat formation around the CCTV screen behind the cashier's desk. Although the man is clearly visible in real life, they* watch George as a small black and white shape on the telly. He stays sitting, rubbing his head and fiddling with the contents of his pockets for some time. Staff pay no attention to the beeping and the hollering as cars try and pull up to the petrol pumps. Within minutes, there is gridlock. Drivers' listless faces peer out of windows as they* steer to avoid the huge vagrant. No one gets out to help.

* *

static
rain
cracking
off
concrete

* *

Then a funny thing happens. George's body gives a sudden sharp twist and a sudden sharp jerk, then he jumps to his feet, raising a crooked arm above

Petrolhead George Taylor has cost Asda over £5000 in damages and pilfered petroleum. The 36 year-old has been issued with an Anti-Social Behaviour Order and is now banned from every petrol station within a 12 mile radius of his Eggleston home. Teesside magistrates heard that on 51 different occasions the Petrol Head terrorised staff and shoppers at the filling station at Asda's South Bank store. On several occasions he was aggressive with staff when they* tried to stop him. Initially he would attempt to purchase petroleum, however more recently, as his circumstances have changed and his notoriety grown, he has opted to arrive by night, slashing piping and filling empty soda cans with their contents. Taylor was caught filling containers after making holes in the hoses. Asda night-shift workers said he usually went for unleaded but was happy with four star and diesel. Despite several hours of CCTV footage, showing Taylor guzzling down fuel, when questioned, he denied all charges.

" B E T T E R A BOTTLE IN FRONT OF ME THAN A FRONTAL LOBOTOMY !"

TWICKENHAM · ASHFORD · WEYBRIDGE · CROYDON · REIGATE · CHERTSEY · MOLESEY · SUTTON · RICHMOND his head. Taking a moment to balance, he cocks a leg, bending its stiff knee so he is poised like Kali, blathering and blabbering. Not a sight to see. Then a slow mechanised movement, which quickly gathers pace, he drops into a maniacal dance. Head rolling one way, eyes the other, flailing limbs; the slapping of his bare feet makes a mad din. He turns, makes a stab for a hose and slashes it, releasing a gush of Premium Unleaded.

Eyes pinned, he stares dead on the camera. Pursing his lips into a whistle. There is no sound on the CCTV but the shrill tones penetrate the glass of the kiosk. He staggers forward, stopping in front of the automatic doors. The confused sensor sends them into a frenzy. They* slide half-open, then change their mind with a jerk and slide half-closed, half-open, half-closed, half-open, half-closed so the words of the song George is singing grow louder and dimmer to the listeners inside.

"Loooooooon-atic soooo-ouup, loooooooon-atic soooo-ouup."

George feels trembly. George feels tremendous. He raises his crumpled soda can in an exultant toast, then begins a mad lurch towards the oncoming traffic filing in through the feeder lane that spews it off the A60.

"What the bloody fuck was that?"

"Did you get his picture this time? Did you?"

You don't need to see his face. You know it already. Blessed, a saint, a martyr, a pimp, a nutter, a creep.   "I wouldn't let that psycho touch me."

George strides up the hard shoulder past a quarter-mile tailback, then manoeuvres into the fast lane weaving through the traffic like a pro. For a second he looks wobbly, tho pays no attention to the cars swerving so as not to hit him. He lifts the soda can and takes a series of glugs, feels the 5 Star Unleaded hit his stomach. His ears go boom! Boom! Boom! The sounds of a big brass brand and George can see fireworks and Chinese cockerels with their wings unclipped, he can taste pomegranates and Turkish delight; taste sugar in milk and horsemeat. An anarchist with an ash-smeared face, he sails on a jasper-green Javanese sea populated by gypsy skinnydippers, who clamber onto lilypads for a rest, baring their breasts. Then the sky is filled with Xeroxed flyers with a photo of his own face. REAL GANGSTERS DON'T WEAR JEWELRY. His footsteps crunch on boiled candy sweets, each, an exquisite magical blessing. He supposes it means something and whatever it is makes him start to laugh, pa, ha, ha, ha, ha, ha, ha. Like a toddler, swaying to keep steady. Pa, ha, ha, ha, ha, ha, ha, he goes. Pa, ha, ha, ha, ha, ha, ha. Ha, ha, *the Ape-drunk, who leaps and sings; the Lion-drunk* ha, ha, ha, ha, ha. Pa, ha, ha, ha, ha, ha, ha. Ha, ha, ha, *who is quarrelsome; the Swine-drunk, who is sleepy and* ha, ha, ha, ha. Pa, ha, ha, ha, ha, ha, ha. Ha, ha, ha, ha, *puking; the Sheep-drunk, wise in his own conceit, but unable to speak; the* ha, ha, ha. Ha, ha, ha, ha, ha, ha, ha. Ha, ha, ha, ha, *Monkey-drunk, who drinks himself sober again; the Goat-drunk, who is* ha, ha. Pa, ha, ha, ha, ha, ha, ha. Ha, ha, ha, ha, ha, ha, ha. *lascivious; and the Fox-drunk, who is crafty, like a Dutchman in his cups.* Pa, ha, ha, ha, ha, ha, ha. Pa, ha, ha, ha, ha, ha.

Pa, ha, ha, ha, ha, ha, ha,
ha, ha, Pa, ha, ha, ha, ha
ha, ha, Pa, ha, ha, ha,
ha, ha,
ha, ha,
ha

THE UNIVERSE WANTS TO PLAY

All characters appearing in this work are fictitious but their resemblance to real persons, both living and dead, is <u>not</u> coincidental. When is it ever?

"Oi. Noel. Mate!"

He'd thought about bringing down his guitar but he'd seen those pricks, leaving home with a battered acoustic over their shoulder. He didn't need that shit. Besides, it made it harder to hop the train. Which he had done. When it pulled in at King's Cross, he'd hung back while everyone else got off, then did a quick rekkie. A few pound coins between seats and a half-full pack of ciggies.

As he steps onto the platform, he clocks the guards. He readies himself with an response but they* pass him without comment, throw suspect glances over shoulders from safe distances. Noel is used to it. He is one of those people everybody stares at. Even when he was sitting sulky and silent in a corner - they* could see him alright.

The station hall is squat and low. Kamikaze pigeons dive-bomb the commuters. They* look odd inside. Noel looks up at the arches in the roof. A giant snowy owl? That can't belong in here. He squints, trying to figure out what a bird like that is doing in a place like this.

"To scare away the pigeons," A guard, who must be near eight foot tall steps up beside him.

Noel stands shoulder to shoulder with the giant facing the crowd, who are staring up at the departures board; a jazzy display of fuzzy orange lettering that ticker tapes. Like sitting under the TV in the pub when the footie's on. Loudspeakers cough into life and begin an announcement so loud that it drowns itself. The train back to Manchester. Folks grab bags and shuffle towards the platform. Somehow they* carry Noel back to the platform edge. He watches new passengers shoehorn themselves into old seats and spread their bags in a passive-aggressive mess. It's a slick operation. The driver hanging from the cabin hollers, waiting for the whistle. Not 12 minutes after it arrived, the train is ready to depart. Cue the last late commuter, waving briefcase, etc. and just catching the door as chug, chug, chug. Back to where it came from. When the red lights blink out in the darkness of the tunnel, Noel turns and walks out the station with a swagger he can't shake.

I live my life in the city
And there's no easy way out
The day's moving just too fast for me
I need some time in the sunshine
I gotta slow it right down
The day's moving just too fast for me
I live my life for the stars that shine
And people say it's just a waste of time
When they said I should feed my head*
Well that to me was just a day in bed
I'll take my car and drive real far
They're not concerned about the way we are
In my mind my dreams are real
Now you concerned about the way I feel

They'd've noticed he was gone by now. But they* wouldn't be worried. On a bender, down the cop shop, over his missus's, dossing on a bench. Everyone happy to judge, never mind that they* were ignorant as shite on the matter.

Engrossed in the minutiae of his family's revolting hypocrisy, Noel puts two winding city miles between him and King's Cross station. He snaps from his reveries at a junction of Kentish Town Road. Gateway to the north. There aren't many places in London grimmer than this. Fraught with horrible histories. The low-slung railway bridge is damp, filth seeping out its bricks, green moss growing under a gush of dirty water that splashes onto the pavement, making puddles or disappearing between paving stones. A road cone sits dauntless on top of a set of traffic lights, but the carnage is leftover, and the streets are dead but for a sweeper who abandons his cart and climbs the steps to a grotty building on one corner. A knocking shop. As the door opens, Noel catches a glimpse of faces so young they* should only belong to teddy bears. *All the dream stealers are lying in wait...* After the door closes, Noel walks on, following the forlorn trajectory of the rubbish cart as it rolls into the gutter. Languid animal-looking thing. He peers inside it and is surprised to find it empty.

The road becomes a high street, shutting up for the night. A hardware shop where a row of drills swing in the window, makes Noel think of chicken. The Abbey Tavern, Day Lewis Pharmacy. Up ahead, a wan yellow glow. Best Kentish Town Kebab. There are three men up on its roof arguing loudly in a language Noel doesn't know, but the shop itself is empty. Through the back wall comes the sound of chaos. Popping champagne corks. The hot plates and fridges are full of food - freshly made chips, saveloys, sausage rolls - and the kebab skewer is fat with sweating meat, but the hairy man behind the counter just stands shaking his head.

"No, no, no, no, no, no, no."

"I got money."

"Eh. We're closed."

Noel holds up his hands.

"Whatever."

He backs out the door to the sound of violins; makes believe he hadn't been hungry in the first place.

Sma Hlink Dry Cleaners, Carpetright, Chicken Cottage, Job Centre, Annie's Bar. Eventually the high street dies away. The pavement gets wider, returning to the what it must've been 40 or 50 years ago. He spots a dimpled church, hidden in shadows. Not one with a soaring steeple, but a fat building, as appetising as a gingerbread house. Noel's beady eye spots something glistening, and he is surprised to see a heavy padlock hanging off a thick set of chains securing the door.

I'd like to be somebody else and not know where I've been
I'd like to build myself a house out of plasticine...
Shake along with me....Shake along with me
I've been driving in my car with my friend Mr Soft
Mr Clean and Mr Ben are living in my loft....
Shake along with me...Shake along with them....
I'm sorry but I just don't know I know, I said I told you so
But when you're happy and you're feeling fine
Then you'll know when it's the right time..

Hampstead Heath (as closely related to the city around it as man is to nature) can be felt before it can be seen. Its silence is a vacuum that pulls you towards it at the same time as it repels you away. The absence of static from TV aerials and the gushing of sewage out of people's homes. It begins abruptly. One moment, boutiques and bakeries - shuttered up for the night - line both sides of the street, then there is black. No streetlights, just a thick line of trees blocking a rising moon. Noel crosses over. He walks on the pavement until a path cuts into the grass. He turns with it. It leads him to the edges of a low black lake. He can only see how big it is because on its far side, warm squares of light thrown out by living room windows are reflected. Some sort of trip, because to Noel's reckoning, there had been no houses for a good ½ mile. Looking down, Noel realises he is standing in sand.

He steps back onto the path. It curls around the lake, then becomes a bridge. Standing here, Noel spots a diving board. It looks more like a pond. Well manky. Away from the water, the path climbs a hill. It disintegrates into a shiny sheet of blackness…then reappears again at a distance…then disintegrates… and so on. Noel abandons that route, and sets off through ditches and swathes of grass so high he has to ford them like water. He clambers over fallen tree trunks and shuffles underneath dropped canopies. It is absurd that there is a place like this here. He wonders if he has walked to the end of the city, or if somewhere in that or that direction London starts again. Poured concrete, spaghetti junctions and warehouses, like what surrounds every urban sprawl. He can't imagine.

Perhaps it isn't chance, but it is certainly a surprise to reach the top of Parliament Hill and find the city bang in front of him again. And didn't it look something. A Whittington welcome! Twinkling tower blocks rise to meet a smart navy sky. Tunnelling lights and blinking headlamps and a warped chorus of beeps, toots and sirens. To Noel it sounds like nightingales.

Maybe I don't really wanna know
how your garden grows
cos I just wanna fly
Lately did you ever feel the pain
in the morning rain
as it soaks you to the bone

Well before the sun comes up, it gets misty. When the first dogwalkers appear, Noel pulls his coat a little tighter, shivering under the stares of north London neo-liberals. He abandons his post and slopes back down the hill, to where the trees grow closer together. It's hard to choose a spot. (Not in a dip.) Then he clocks something. It is, unmistakably, a corner. Dusty yellow brick, Noel imagines it must've been grand.

Before he lies down, he goes through his pockets taking out what money he's got. He takes off his rings too, then his shoes and puts everything in his socks, then puts his shoes back on and ties the laces.

Though utterly hidden, he has a perfect view across the meadow that leads up to the hill. He presses his back squarely against his corner, crooks one arm under his head and thinking 'Tomorrow!' falls asleep.

Hey you, up in the sky, learning to fly,
tell me how high
Do you think you'll go
Before you start fall
ing
Hey you! Up in a tree, you wanna be me, well that couldn't
be
Cos the people here
they don't hear you calling
How does it feel when you're inside me?
How does it feel when you're inside?

When Noel wakes, it's duller. And cooler. He is happy lying on the ground, and stays there for some time. Only when the hunger in his belly becomes acute does he remember the row of shops at the edge of the heath. He gets to his feet. Back to reality. Give something a shot. As he walks, he brushes his parka clean of the fine dust mud makes when it dries.

A thin rain starts to fall. On common land it makes everything look fantastic, but as soon as he steps into concrete, the drizzle is annoying. He darts between shop canopies to keep dry but finds it impossible to stay in step with the shoppers' slow crawl. He bumps into backs and steps on toes.

"Sorry," he mutters, to disgusted old ladies.

They* duck his gaze and refuse him before he can carry on talking.

"No. No. Sorry. Just, no."

*There we were now here we are. All this confusion nothing's the same to me. There we were now here we are. All this confusion nothing's the same to me. I can't tell you the way I feel Because the way I feel is oh so new to me I can't tell you the way I feel Because the way I feel is oh so! new to me What I heard is not what I hear I can see the signs but they're not very clear What I heard is not what I hear. I can see the signs but they're not very clear. So I can't tell you the way I feel Because the way I feel is oh so new to me. I can't tell you the way I feel Because the way I feel is oh so new to me.
This is confusion, am I confusing you?*

The Kentish Town job centre is an exercise in oppression. Everything here, including the walls, began life flat-pack. Posters of shiny black people against shocking yellow backgrounds shout in bold blue print: APPLY THE SKILL SET YOU NEVER KNEW YOU HAD.

Noel shuffles the crappy print-outs of vacancies between his fingers like a pack of cards. He hasn't read them, just run off the first few. No. 164. He walks up to the desk but before he can sit down, a woman's voice behind him says,

"Could you come through to the back?"

Noel is shown into a room and left alone to listen to the shuffle of feet along the linoleum corridor outside. Pale ferns deprived of sunlight sag sadly on the desk in front of him. Everything is dirty. The walls are dirty and the click floorboarding is dirty, the carpets are dirty, the chairs and sofas are dirty, highlighted by unforgiving strip lighting. Behind him, someone opens a door. The mad rattle of the air conditioning clicks off for a second, then a hum and it comes back on again.

"First time signing on?"

A blonde slides soundlessly into the chair on the other side of the desk. Dirty suit. Blank, grey irises.

"Yeah."

"So exactly what type of work are you looking for Mr Gallagher?"

The look she gives him - the old Noel'd've had the desk against the wall, magazines scattered across the floor, in seconds. She speaks through her nose,

"There are a several vacancies here waiting to be filled."

I need to be myself. I can't be no one else.
I'm feeling supersonic. Give me gin and tonic.
You can have it all, but how much do you want it?
You make me laugh. Give me your autograph.
Can I ride with you in your B.M.W.?
You can sail with me in my yellow submarine.
You need to find out, cos no one's gonna tell you what I'm on
about. You need to find a way for what you want to say. But
before tomorrow. Cos my friend said he'd take you home. Sits
in a corner all alone. He lives under a waterfall. Nobody can
see him. Nobody can ever hear him call.

The Housing Options Office: Even more oppressive than the Dole.

"You will have to have been living in the area for 3 months in order to apply to be put on the housing waiting list."

Cos that makes sense.

The woman who speaks to him through the bulletproof glass – where does this place think it is? – does not even look up from her Top Tips for Top Barnets.

"Egg yolk," Noel offers. "Works better than all that junk, and it's good as free."

The words apparently sit so far out of the woman's frame of reference, they* fall on deaf ears. Noel takes his ticket, then turns to contemplate the waiting room (a large Hindustani family, the mother in tears and a deranged old drunk in a game of one-upmanship, similarly bawling his eyes out), then makes straight for the door. It is only to his retreating back that the woman looks up and whispers.

"You'll have a long wait luv."

Whas that sound ringing around your brain?
Today was just a blur, you gotta head like a ghost train.
What was that sound ringing around your brain?
You're here on your own who you gonna find to blame?
You're the outcast, you're the underclass,
But you don't care, because you're living fast.
You're the uninvited guest who stays 'till the end
I know you've got a problem that the devil sent
You think they're talking 'bout you but you dunno who
I'll be scraping yourass from the sole of my shoe tonight.

The pub is warm and Noel is almost tempted to spend the £3.20 rattling in his pocket on a pint rather than skulk at the end of the bar empty-handed while the manager is sought. The reply comes in the sort of clipped, measured tones reserved for stupid little boys.

"You will find our serving staff are a little more freshly… kempt," the man sneers, eyeing the chip missing from Noel's ear.

(Noel has not for a second considered how the last week sleeping on the heath has affected his appearance.)

"I'll have a Guinness then. Prick."

Is it my imagination or have I finally found something worth living for?
I was lookin for some action but all I found was cigarettes and alcohol
You could wait for a lifetime
To spend your days in the sunshine
You might as well do the white line

Cos when it comes on top . . .
You gotta make it happennn,
You gotta make it happen.
Is it worth the aggravation to find yourself a job when there's
nothing worth working for ?
It's a crazy situation but all I need are cigarettes and alcohol.
You could wait for a lifetime
To spend your days in the sunshine
You might as well do the white line
Cos when it comes on top . . .
You gotta make it happennn,
You gotta make it happen.

Outside a hardware shop. Tidy squares of black tarpaulin, on offer for a pound a pop. One slips inside Noel's coat. A few blocks further, in more residential climes, a saggy-bottomed seat has been left outside a garage door. Might as well. Noel slings it over his shoulder easily. Adding a stained, but completely dry pair of quilts (found folded on top of a rubbish bin) to his load, Noel makes his way towards the heath.

This time it is with a familiarity that is still a long way off contempt. that he crosses the open plains and dirty ditches, now noticing details on the floor and patterns in the scenery that he had missed before. Avoiding Parliament Hill (he has had enough of the city in all its guises) he makes a beeline for his corner.

He hadn't felt a wind but unfolding the tarp tells different. It is flapping around like a mad thing, but after some minutes of struggle Noel manages to secure one corner with a stone, then another. He lifts the material over two large bushes and pins the other two corners into the ground with twigs. Having formed these makeshift digs, he shoves the chair under, tosses in the blankets then crawls in after. It is funny inside. The light is eerie, but nothing compared to the noises: whistles, scratching and ripping. Was that a rip? He gropes blindly for the chair. Clambering up on it, he laughs as the "ceiling", low as it is, wraps itself around his face.

What a life it would be
If you would come to mine for tea
I'll pick you up at half past three
And we'll have lasagne.
I'll treat you like a Queen
I'll feed you strawberries and cream
Then your friends will all go green
For my lasagne.
These could be the best days of our lives
But I don't think we've been living very wise, I said

Oh no, no, no, no. He unfolds one of the quilts and lays it on the ground. Wrapping the second around his head and shoulders, he lies down… to sleep. This time not so well… His misadventures in the city paw miserably at his dreams, dissipating only when he wakes to the first drops of rain drumming down on the tarp. Now a sense of satisfaction creeps over Noel. He lies, drifting in and out of dreams for the whole of the morning, until a warm autumn takes over the day and lures him out into it. Coughing and stamping to shake out the damp, Noel rubs his hands together and eyes his creation. There are problems with it, that is for sure, but to Noel's systematic mind at least, it seems a decision has been made.

Slide away, and give it all you've got
My today, fell in from the top
I dream of you, and all the things you say
I wonder where you are now.
Hold me down all the world's asleep
I need you now, you knocked me off my feet,
I dream of you and we talk of growing old
But you said please don't…
Slide away baby, together we'll fly
I've tried praying, but I don't know what you're saying to me
Now that you're mine
We'll find a way
Chasing the sun
Let me be the one, that shines with you
In the morning, I don't know what to do
We're two of a kind
We'll find a way
Chasing the sun.

He envisions a warm fireside and a rocking chair. Like as had been at his Nan's flat. A country cottage at the top of a tower block. He sees a vegetable patch and some sort of contraption for capturing water. Of course electricity was going to be a problem but then -

Everything centers around the wall, a lagging empire, soon to be reinstated by grace of his hand. Every day he walks through town, and so stuff begins to accumulate. The first find is a sash window, taken out of its wall complete with frame; no doubt replaced with some double-glazing contraption. The second, a series of upturned apple crates. (If these sound too antiquated and idyllic, it is because they* are pilfered from outside a Hampstead Village delicatessen. On sale for £17.99 to complete 'that rustic look' that organic ash-rind cheese brings to every kitchen.) Cardboard boxes, a set of brown corduroy cushions, an empty keg, a sprung foldable camp bed and a leather office chair discarded for a small rip in its seat; the first two steps of an old wooden staircase, a wall compass and slabs of mirrored glass. A lamp is lugged hopefully for hours before Noel re-realises his situation. (Londoners eye him suspiciously as he lays the thing down in the middle of the high street with as much purpose as he can muster.) A blackboard, complete with chalk taped to its back, armfuls of bin liners and plastic bags, gaffer tape - he waterproofs everything. Tupperware boxes, empty soda cans (good for candles), the stubs of broken knives, a clock, which turns out to be a barometer, so far more useful, and a guitar. The contents of a skip provide seven sheets of hard, candy-coloured plastic, some disintegrating bricks and flimsy strips of balsa wood. The plastic is perfect for flooring, the wood, for shelves. A framed photograph of Rodney Marsh, found rotting behind some bins takes pride of place between two scrumpled old posters; one a film poster of The Good, the Bad and the Ugly and another of Burt Bacarach.

Days pass and early mornings start to get colder. Foraging lapses, and building begins in earnest.

Noel maps out three rooms on either side of a small courtyard. The first room he builds out of corrugated iron, nicked off the back of a tinker truck left in a heath car park overnight. This room has a roof and a chimney and a hole dug in the floor to use as a safe.

The second room is less sturdy, incorporating a tree; it is more of makeshift tent. This windswept room is where Noel puts his bed (a pile of so many broken mattresses that their individual uncomfortableness is negated). He uses the tree to hang his clothes, as well as pots and pans and birdfood.

The third room is made of glass; one wall is the sash-window found on the first raid, another shards of smashed stained glass; red and blue; their points jammed into soil. This room has no roof. Instead, Noel sits an armchair beneath a mandala of torn umbrellas; a sentient spot where he spends almost all his time. On the ground, circling the seat, wide-necked bottles and tubs collect rainwater.

By the time the cold sets in, the house is complete. It is just liked what he'd dreamed of. Better. Forget Supernova Heights! he thinks, Noel has built himself an oasis.

There's no need for you to say you're sorry
Goodbye I'm going home
I don't care no more so don't you worry
Goodbye I'm going home
I hate the way that even though you know you're wrong You say you're right
I hate the books you read and all your friends

Your music's shite it keeps me up all night, up all night
There's no need for you to say you're sorry
Goodbye I'm going home
I don't care no more so don't you worry
Goodbye I'm going home
I hate the way that you are so sarcastic
And you're not very bright
You think that everything you've done's fantastic
Your music's shite it keeps me up all night, up all night
And it will be nice to be alone
For a week or two
But I know that I will be back
Right back here with you, with you, with you, with you, with you,
with you, with you...
There's no need for you to say you're sorry
Goodbye I'm going home
I don't care no more so don't you worry
Goodbye
I'm going home...

TRAMP GIVEN £2M HAMPSTEAD HEATH PLOT AFTER SQUATTING FOR 20 YEARS

24 MAY

Home for Noel Gallagher is a rickety shack surrounded by junk. Yet this man, who calls his home his "oasis" is the unlikeliest of property millionaires. Noel has become the proud owner of a prime plot of land on the edge of Hampstead Heath. According to squatters' rights, that Noel has lived in his self-made mansion longer than the 12 years required by law means he has been declared the ground's legal owner.

The plot, which consists of a 90ft square woodland area around a 12ftx8ft shack has been Mr Gallagher's home since 1992. If it were sold estate agents say it would fetch more than £20million, but Mr Gallagher says he has no intention of cashing in. Yesterday, after a visit to the shops with his plastic bag hanging from an umbrella slung across his shoulder, he said of his decision to live here:

"There's only so many times you can stand in your kitchen talking about David Icke and the f***ing pyramids..."

Bizarrely it was an attempt to evict Noel that led to his owning the land. Proceedings began in March 2005, but the case was dropped after his solicitors presented evidence of the length of his residence. Throughout proceedings, Gallagher was evasive. "Definitely Maybe," he said. Courts were able to contact a Liam Gallagher living with his mum outside Salford, however there seems to be no love lost between the two. "It takes more than blood to me brother," was all the other Gallagher had to say. *(Too fucking right - Ed.)*

> To make media the centre of life, means to live a mediated existence.

HEAVY VIBRATIONS

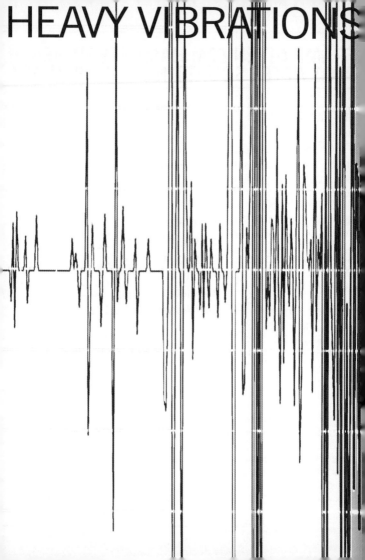

Just like how nothing ever changes, nothing has changed. The planets aligned, the comets rained down, followed by the prophets; the Age of Enlightenment came and went and now, it's been clear to everyone for a long time, that this bit is over. For a second, it'd looked like everything, as Bob Marley had said it would be, was going to be alright. There was a love in the universe, and what's more, it formed a pattern! Human beings were made in the shape of God - it wasn't just projection. Hallelujah. Only wait. Human beings were formed in the shape of God. And so despite epiphanies being donated free of charge to any stoned soul willing to climb a mountain, the application of these ideas was only implemented after a long hiatus or the maximum amount of misaction. Slogans of counterculturalists and voices of dissent no longer preached LOVE & RESPECT as the key to success; BLOOD & FIRE! The old fortune teller lies dead on the floor and the world over, women are giving birth to twins; Haile and Kylie being the most common names - parents banking on the teaching of any one of the prophets to guard and guide their child to stardom. Ever since the theological debate was essentially shut down - about four years after schools started teaching science and art as a single subject again, which prompted the discovery in 2016, that there was a G-d, it was a particle (and that the Jews were right, it didn't like being spelt out) - everyone's been waiting.

Jesus is late.

The oracle box has a tight schedule these days. Daytime shows hold host to miserable 20-somethings, who each had their turn thinking they were the 2nd coming of the Messiah and are now largely ruined, living in empty Dalston loft spaces. Early evening watching is dominated by talent shows which scour Africa looking for the next big thing. Shoeless teenagers queue in sandy streets, waiting for their five minutes in front of the judges.

Next we have Momodo Limini Ntchek. An 11 year-old from Senegal. Momo fused two fingers on his left hand together a year ago, while working for Gambian Telecom Communications and received no pay out. An orphan since the age of six - the cameras zoom in on Momodo, focusing on his left eye, blurring into the black of his pupil and scanning the ID card nestled in his optic nerve, opening a sequence of POV clips: of Momodo being born, of his father's funeral, of Momodo losing his fingers, of Momodo in the Lighthouse Chapel where he speaks in tongues to a congregation of fat mixed race sociopaths, screaming their hakuna matatas.

In the late hours, the global channel (Americanised as it is) does provide some good commentary. TV producers reap the inner-city ghettos of half the world, from south Detroit to Peckham Rye, picking out bruised fruit and

heroin importers who can't cry. Preachermen - once exiled to subscription only channels 11034-12977 - are now primetime. Ball-eyed women scream the news. *Mi hear an inspirational story just other day bout a poverty-stricken yute, born in the streets of Philadelphia. When he is only likkle he misspend his days, chilling out and getting in fights with boys on de playground who were up to no good, started making trouble in his living....area. Lord speed him out to his rich arenty and uncle, across in the most peaceful area of Bel Air... I think there are some gremlins in the system?*

It's from a comedy show, a voice off camera says.

And because everyone is on TV, everyone watches TV, and believes in it (not like in the olden days, where certain types would proudly proclaim "I don't have a telly" tho be streaming shows 24-7. You weren't anybody if you weren't downloading something...) Content is a free for all. Because essentially there is no authority, questioning authority no longer poses any threat to authority. There is no longer any balance between good and evil. From the pragmatist to the most extreme conspiracy theorist - if pro-active enough - anyone can get a voice. (What better way to disarm a man than by letting him get his point across?) As vague as it is, sublime authority simply assimilates dissent. *Black people in the west have been franchised and no longer object to the system - however right-wing - hence the liberal left - who looked to the black majority for the lead on their own political stance, and are the chief activist political force - are similarly lost.* The philosophy can only be aspirational. The only thing that can happen now is that something becomes so evil, it destroys itself. See previous world governments, inter-national NGOs and mega churches - cos the best thing Satan ever did was to persuade us that he doesn't exist. And Everybody knows that this time round, it won't be some persecuted soul in bondage, under sufferation, enslaved. The second coming will be the fucking anti-Christ.

[Revelations 17: 18] And the woman which thou sawest is that great city, which reigneth over the kings of the earth.

40 Es in a night.

[Revelations 17: 15] And upon her forehead was a name written, mystery, Babylon the Great, the mother of harlots and abominations of the earth.

Wears Lynx Africa.

[Revelations 18: 24] And in her was found the blood of prophets, and of saints, and of all that were slain upon the earth.

Trainer fetish.

[Revelations 18: 1] And after these things I saw another angel come down from heaven, having great power; and the earth was lightened with his glory.

Sells drugs.

[Revelations 19: 12] His eyes were as a flame of fire, and on his head were many crowns; and he had a name written, that no man knew, but he himself.

Chancer, nutter; no hope.

[Revelations 18: 2] And he cried mightily with a strong voice, saying, Babylon the great is fallen, is fallen, and is become the habitation of devils, and the hold of every foul spirit, and a cage of every unclean and hateful bird.

No ghetto sob story, where there was no other way, like how Yardies get sent out of Kingston.

[Revelations 18: 3] For all nations have drunk of the wine of the wrath of her fornication, and the kings of the earth have committed fornication with her, and the merchants of the earth are waxed rich through the abundance of her delicacies.

No Pablo Escobar either.

[Revelations 18: 7] How much she hath glorified herself, and lived deliciously, so much torment and sorrow give her: for she saith in her heart, I sit a queen, and am no widow, and shall see no sorrow.

A middle class kid that drops his t's when he asks for the butter.

[Revelations 18: 8] Therefore shall her plagues come in one day, death, and mourning, and famine; and she shall be utterly burned with fire: for strong is the Lord God who judgeth her.

Always buys the drinks.

[Revelations 18: 14] And the fruits that thy soul lusted after are departed from thee, and all things which were dainty and goodly are departed and thou shalt find them no more at all.

For ego, for status, for fun.

[Revelations 18: 9] And the kings of the earth, who have committed fornication and lived deliciously with her, shall bewail her, and lament for her, when they shall see the smoke of her burning.

It's a fucking joke.

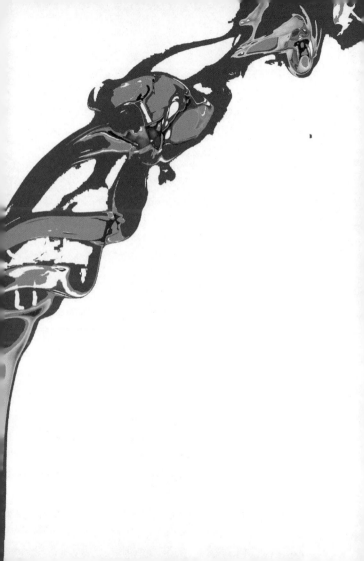

TOPSHOP
RETURNS

FIRE 'PON DEM

Up until recently, I'd thought I was the only person who lived the way I do. Arguably a forced circumstance, its weakness is also its strength. Mi nah bow down for mi money. Which mostly means I don't have any. Money, that is. And so there have not been many moments where I have fallen victim to the casual abuse of corporate and consumerist culture. But it did happen once. **Mašá Alláh.**

I cannot recall the exact details of how I came about the £370 in my pocket, nor how I came to be on a bus that stopped at Oxford Circus in the middle of the day. This is where I went to school, learned how to shoplift and practised smoking fags. Nipping between buses, which go so slow, terrorising the length and breadth. These days I usually avoid it, despising the competition and desperation that gets right up in your face - tho even I have to admit that the new crossing is spot on. A proper bit of town planning. In the old days, eight sets of traffic lights went red an' green in turn, but they* might as well have flashed forever yellow. It was constant gridlock, people weaving between shuddering engines and bastard beeps. Today's is a more totalitarian approach (the only way to deal with the masses - Ed.). All traffic stops and people flood the road, crossing at diagonals. There is enough space for a 10-strong barricade of teenage girls with their arms linked to stroll on and present no problem to others. I am standing and watching exactly this, when a boy catches my eye. He smiles and I turn away to find myself facing a huge TV screen broadcasting heavily stylised substance abuse. Images that looked like they* could be by Deren, and that's the point. Underneath the TV, five escalators churn away. I'm through the door before I know I've done it. With my second step, my feet are on the conveyor belt and I am carried down into the belly of the beast. Bright lights and good mirrors show up the yellowness of my skin. As I get to the bottom, I realise that there are no escalators back up. They* are somewhere... over there...on the other side of a mountain of leopard print pumps, jazzy jeggings and standardised vintage finds, then a sea of multicolour denim. I have to brave it, and so... Heads down, bottoms up? More like elbows out, winding my way through rotating rails that grab at my clothes as if they* want to tear them off. 'One of us, one of us.' It takes me 15 minutes to escape, and I think I get away lightly. I find myself outside, trembling, a shoebox clutched under my arm, inside a pair of stilettos. No bag (too embarrassing). Razor-sharp heel, pointed toes, you wanna know what colour they* were? Cos if you do - fuck off.

I carried them back to mine and tried them on again, this time for long enough to realise how painful they* are and how impossible to walk in. I stand in front of the mirror, looking at the slick arch of my foot with mild concern for the safety of my ankles, and the radio starts talking about it.

"If you look at a man wiz no clothes on wearing shoes, you sink 'there is a man wiz only his shoes on' but you look at a woman wizout clothes but wiz shoes on and you have before you a naked woman."

I take my clothes off, then put the heels on again. Now I can clearly see what they* was trying to say, and that was the point. My tits and bum forced up and out, the small of my back curved in. I look at the reflection of my feet. The radio was wrong. I wrapped my arms around my torso like a straitjacket, then squatted down on my haunches, feeling the points of the heels dig into the carpet as I swung back on my ankles. Through stoned eyes I looked at a black girl's pussy, sullen and bruised, and a pink more shocking than any shocking pink on the in.

RETURN WITHIN 28 DAYS

I had to take them back. It took me 26 days to cement the resolve to return, but did it I did. Hood up. Grim face. I get off the bus a stop too late and have to fight my way through a crowd where everyone is walking towards me except for the occasional very slow elderly couple, blocking the way. Shopping lollers drool, tongues against windows. Fucking Forrest Gumps. Push past 'em. Everyone is excuse me excuse me. They* are short. I look up at the tops of arcades and the sky, brace myself and barge through, not caring who I walk into. I am making fast progress when I see someone else doing sort of the same thing. A Rasta man. Taller than everyone else. Every bit of him looks like it's been hurt. Dusty man. Dressed in clothes like you don't see anymore. Fatigues? Matted greens and woven khakis, an enormous old army sack slung over his back. Balding, but looking more tortured than old. He is talking down at the tops of people's heads, his hands making silent blessings in the air.

"There is another way. There is another way." He keeps repeating himself. "There is another way."

I can hear you. I whisper it. We are still a way away from each other and there is no way he can actually hear me, but still he turns - maybe only because I have my eyes pinned on him and he can feel it. I smile. He doesn't, he's busy. He nods and moves on. He's not after the converts. Not when there were so many sinners about.

T**S**p is spelt out in lights. I walk in like a soldier. With a little bit of Rasta. I find I am able to block everything out. I can't hear the shit tunes, can't see the idiots, am walking through a nothing that isn't even there. I eye up each bored boyfriend, collecting as many snarls as I can. Lingering in the lingerie losers.

"Returns. I want. Returns."

"Downstairs. At the back."

T**S**p Returns is amazing! An undisguised slur on its users; so horrible in fact that most T**S**ppers cannot bear to picture themselves in there, scared that the peeling walls and naked floorboards possess some poetic irony that will force their fate closer to ending up in a dingy crack hole with an alcoholic boyfriend and two kids by different fathers, one deceased. Er... Next to the toilets, stinking of piss, the corner bears witness to some of Taiwanese sweatshops' most ambitious mistakes - size 24 striped hot pant dungarees, luminous green half nylon half fake fur bomber jacket, chequered pink flat caps with AC/DC patches. Atrocities waiting to get sent to Primark's dispatches warehouse for a second chance at half price.

Though the queue is short, it is long.

"What the fuck is with this place?"

Everyone is kicking off. Shuffling their feet. Arguing. Telling someone else to shut up. RAH! Eventually I get a till, a Bangladeshi boy. Either a rudeboy turned goody-goody, or just a mumma's boy. Hard to tell.

"They* try and make it as grim as possible in here huh?"

He looks at me, says nothing, but I can see his eyes.

"Like, what's that smell?"

He beeps the tag on my shoe box. He shrugs.

He opens the box and I breathe in as he takes the shoes out and looks at the bottoms. Bit scuffed. He disappears with them into the stockroom. I turn and eye the girls in the queue behind me and grin. When he comes back, he doesn't say anything.

"Is that cool?"

"Yup," he is as curt as he can be. He pings open the till and counts out thirteen tens.

"You got a pound?"

"No."

He slaps the money down on the desk.

"Forget about it."

I take the money.

"Cheers. See ya."

He bangs the till shut and a receipt reels off the printer.

"Just fill this in."

I lean over to sign a fake name. Pen poised in hand I say, "They* don't even let you listen to music in here huh?"

For a second he is quiet, he looks tired and bored. He stares me out for a second (rudeboy!), then he starts to laugh, he bangs his hands down on the counter and laughs some more, starts to shake his head, looks relieved.

"Nah...we can have music in here if we want," he says, "only we leave it off cos it's all so fucking shit."

Bun down the walls of Babylon and dem evil concept junkies

JUDGEMENT

The Wanker

When he had thought about it, he assumed that the way his prick made him feel would make him more kindly inclined towards its appearance. The thick base stapled into groin, the tired curve at its middle, the polite hood at the end. All of it repulsed him. Stepping out the shower and watching its mad swing, hanging from the loose skin of his scrotum, the dark colourless hair that clung wetly alongside it, bore no relevance to the thrill and longing tugging on it could engender. Sometimes, when it was hard he would glimpse down hoping that some transformation had occurred, hoping to find some smooth menace worthy of the rest of him. Golden boy.

Despite his distaste for his penis, it was with some concern that he noticed the first small changes. Two bumps, on the left and right sides, half way up, or down. Depending on how you looked at it. He guided careful fingers across them. It was hard to tell if they* were actually A Thing, as the slightest pressure soothed them back to nothing.

Stumbling his way to the toilet in the early hours of the morning, fumbling to find the string and tugging downwards to ping the light on, eyes half closed at the brightness, flipping the toilet seat up, it landing against the wall with a clatter at the same time as piss jetted out of him in an anarchic trajectory. All over the bathroom floor.

'Fuck -'

He looks down to inspect the offending organ to see its end caked in cracked dry cum. Trying to ease the peeing, he pulls back the foreskin and peels off a portion of settled semen. He squeezes the tip. Inside is wet and slimy. He looks away. Right at the light. Bollocks. 3 dark patches block his vision. He sees himself in the mirror, gormless, standing with his cock in his hand. Idiot. He looks down. It winks. He twangs off the bathroom light and makes his way back to bed, feeling blindly at dark air.

Most weeks he would waste away indoors. Wake up, morning wank, on computer, cups of tea, then to work (strictly amateur), get diverted by the internet, get annoyed, off computer, maybe some food… The cycle would repeat itself in endlessly shifting shifts, monitored by the ringing of the bell from the school next door and the screams from the playground. He always woke at 8.30, 10.20, 12.40 or 3.30. Sometimes it was hard to tell one from the other. Sometimes he would potter about his house long into the night, sleeping at 4am. Other times, he would be tired out by half past 7, pass out on the sofa, wake at 3am, go to bed and lie there 'til it got light, followed by a couple of hours kip.

This morning, he wakes to his phone's ring. It's The Pest. His best mate.

"Yes boy!"

The Pest has a new squeeze.

"Her place is two minutes from you."

This wouldn't mean much, except the chiquita doesn't

speak much English and comes complete with an entourage of fellow foreigners who chatter on endlessly in Espanol.

"Need a spot of the Queen's Finest from time to time."

The girls had put on breakfast:

"We've got French toast on the go. Bacon, maple syrup, the lot."

He's there.

He hangs up.

Three missed calls. Five texts. Standard.

Hey, i'm sorry 4 acting like such a freak. x

Talk to me! I just wanna see u. Don't do this!

U know what? Fuck u. Go play your power games with someone else.

Since when did you become such a soulless motherfucker?

Baby. I'm sorry. R U OK?

Reading them makes him tired. He lies back in bed. Fucking psycho. The whole thing is so over. Still, thinking about her, he gets a semi, remembering leaning her over the bonnet of his car at the side of the road in Cornwall. Fuck, he had hated her that day...The phone beeps and despite himself, he checks it.

I've always thought that it's ok to be a slut 4 a big dick.

Paha. As he gets dressed, he recalls the night's misadventure in the dreamy fashion of all reminisces of 3ams.　　»　　　»　　　»　　　»　　　Vaguely.

Check for keys, phone, money and music, double check keys then bowl out.

The Spanish live almost on the same block, but in a smart new-build, whose initial glass-partitioned promise gives way to the reality of whitewashed MDF.

The Pest welcomes him in, Super Tennent's in hand.

"Goes down well in the morning."

While food is being cooked, he loiters by the fridge watching the girls squeal and play fight, whilst eyeing up the photos covering the fridge, hundreds of shots of the same nubile flesh twisted in poses stolen from fashion magazines; pouts and/or over-zealous gestures of ecstasy.

After breakfast, it is time for ketamine and computers. Videos of animals maiming one another and 1980s cartoons battle for pride of place while crumbs of coarse white powder gravitate downwards.

Soon it is dark. The Pest gets a call and walks out the room, talking so loudly in the corridor that everyone else has little choice but to listen.

"7 rigs."

"Mate."

"So you'll come by?"

"There's a few of us."

"It's an old phone exchange in Acton," he says, when he walks back into the room. "Kev's got a van. He'll be outside in 5."

The squat is in an enormous derelict warehouse by the Grand Union canal. There are only five sound systems, and one of them doesn't turn on at all, despite the attempts of rave monkeys clambering over it 'til the early hours. Two of the others are techno, but one set up in the basement, where water pours down the walls, has some old baldheads playing 94 jungle. An assortment of black-faced ravers and their dreadlocked counterparts collect between collapsed walls and mashed up storage containers. The other rig has set up on the top floor churning out breakbeat. Dreads and scallies leap about behind the decks, taking turns on the mic. *A shout out to my toilet crew. STILL LOCKED UP!* The rest of the complex is empty, even with the 400 Lost-It's wandering about. And freezing fucking cold: There is only one way forward. Drugs and dancing work so well that they* don't notice when the sun comes up, so it is a complete surprise when they* venture outside that it is a glorious day. Crazy-faces bop about. The crew stroll through the chaos, and stop at a spot on the bridge over the canal. There are loads of Spanish about, so the girls prove useful in sourcing sips and bumps. Further along the banks, a circus of crusties are cavorting. One plays Poi. Another is on the bongos. Girls in sari trousers turn cartwheels on the grass. One tie-dyed adventurer climbs up onto railings that run beside the water. He lets go with his hands, balancing as he tries to stand.

"Way! Wahey!"

He wobbles and sways. It's like a cartoon.

"'Ey, guys, guys, eh."

He is standing, proud. He begins to walk, just keeping his balancing, when a tight-knit pack of hoods appear on the path behind him. Had they* been at the rave? There was no other reason they* would be out here. Then again, rudeboys have a strange way of turning up places.

Everyone else is covered in a thin layer of grime, their trainers sticky with rave juice, but these kids are pristine: All in uniform, looking like black panthers, threading through the crowd in single file. And they* don't do anything. Everyone saw from where they* sat. They* don't touch him. They* just slink by. And somehow the hippy falls. He doesn't tumble tho - he sails in an arc, headfirst underwater. As if he dived. The rudeboys don't even look. Everyone else does, and they* see the guy surface, black and shiny with engine oil, his wet dreads like a giant clump of seaweed slapped on top his head. And underneath, a slash of crimson. He doesn't appear to realise. He swims. Even from far away, you can see his wild eyes. They are popping out his skull. He reaches shore, climbs out onto the bank and then he runs, screaming a mad gabble that can be heard long after he is out of sight. One repeated word that sounds like Caligula - but what would that mean? 10 minutes later a helicopter flies in.

"It must be for him."

Another 12 and pandas arrive. The police are ominously unconfrontational: They* wander through the carnage without speaking to anyone, but their presence is enough for paranoia to set in. Grams burn holes in pockets.

"Never tell me not to be paranoid. Paranoia is boom. Paranoia saves lives."

The Tube is open. Now seems as good a time as any. They* exit as a massive crew and somehow end up back at his, where they* make cheese on toast, slowly.

"Sorry, but do you have any vegan cheese?"

"Piss off mate."

"Who the fuck are these people?"

The Pest points round the room at various reprobates chewing on bread and cheeks.

"Ed, Sam, Dave, Squinx, Kev, Disney, Flakes, Marcus -" the front door opens, "Oli!"

Plastic bags bugling with Stellas are held aloft.

"Fuck it, go on then."

"And I got you your milk."

The Pest grabs the half pint, opens it and drinks.

"Helps with the acid indigestion," he says cheerily, offering it around.

There is a girl in his bed. He can't tell who. Spoon a stranger. His head is cotton-woolly; he climbs in and wraps his arm around her. As he drifts to sleep, he can hear people shuffling about and The Pest launching into a stream of consciousness from underneath the stack of pillows he is using like a blanket.

"Blah, blah, blah, tomorrow," his hopeful little voice says.

The following day's hangover makes him lose all free will, and somehow the next two weeks become one long hang out; a charge between pubs and parties and back seats of cars, all to a constant stream of shit chat, reliving events that have just happened where everyone present was present.

"They* found him in the car park covered in shit."

"Yea, with his trousers round his ankles."

"Tossing himself off."

"He wasn't!"

"If I didn't like reggae so much, I'd probably have a job."

"I'm sorry but if I shat myself, I'd go the fuck home."

"I saw him round the back chasing after these 2 girls who were yelling, 'It's the poo man!'"

"And then that old queen who hadn't realised - 'What do you mean the champagne's arrived?'"

"He was trying to claim that it wasn't his. That he had fallen in someone else's."

"That's even worse!"

It carries on and on and on: to the shops, to the pub, to a park bench, to a sofa, to a house party. When they* pass out, it is in piles, hands shoved down pants or clasping torsos. Out to wait on a street corner for a black Mercedes and a bloke called Devon.

"One leg."

"You're kidding."

Meet new additions at a house halfway across London, to someone's little sister's house, cabs to a club in Vauxhall, you don't get in, to some railway arches with inexcusable wreckheads stumbling round it. Teenage girls start calling your number. Strangers laugh and agree with everything you say.

"Do you think time goes fastest when you are on your back because you are more streamlined to the way the world turns?"

"Deep."

Maybe it was.

Finally, however, there is stuff pressing enough to attend to, and boring enough for the gang not to want to tag along. Rent needs paying, stuff needs putting back in the fridge. He leaves the current line up (at that moment engaged in "trying to buy more k," and getting a girl to come by to give out cheap tattoos.) He attempts 15 'I'm going's' before finally slipping out the front door, down the echoing staircase and into the street. It is freezing out here. Weird, finally being alone. He walks, waiting for the stream of nonsensical conversation to die down and allow his own thoughts to come. All the things he'd said, all the things he'd said, running through my head, running through my head. He watches an old nutter cross a zebra crossing. When the guy gets to the other side and the cars start moving again, he waits to cross back.

"Exactly mate."

Walking into his is depressing. The cold is damp, and the darkness, brown. Flicking one switch turns on three low lamps positioned round the room. Taking two steps backwards, one step forward, he launches himself over the pile of crap on the floor and dives onto his bed. He lies there for a minute, feeling the clammy sheets adjust to his temperature. He feels along the waistband of his jeans then shoves his hand down the front. His prick is soft, but tingling-ly sensitive. It feels swollen and heavy in his hand. Fatter than usual. He pulls his hand out and turns to lie on his back, labouredly unbuttoning his jeans, heaving his hips up to pull them down to his ankles, then finally fighting them off with his feet. He burrows his head into the pillows as his right hand gently holds his dick. One finger catches on something. A hair has twisted round it, that is trapped in the crease of his foreskin. He feels it sliding through the fold. He tries to prize it free, tugs at it, but instead of coming out easily out, he feels a brief, electric pain and the hair stays put. It is rooted. He looks down and sees it is not alone. From the tip, all the way along the underneath runs a thin strip. Not the twangy curls of pubes, nor like the hair on his own head, but the first polite whisps of gold. Slapping his dick up against his belly, he runs a finger down the line of hair, amazed. It's got bigger, that's for sure. And wider, at least at its middle. He can barely close his fingers around it. A new spatter of demure freckles mark the skin at its tip, which he pulls back gently. His japseye stretches to a smile and the thing looks so pretty that he can't help but smile back. He lets go. The skin subsides into a soft pout. He lets it lie against him, reaching up to where his rib cage begins, happy. He is still for a moment, feeling its throb, then starts stroking it lazily.

"Don't stop," he murmurs. "It feels so good."

Then a violence takes over him. He clasps his cock with both hand and - don't think of her... Fuck it - bashes one out.

The next day he can't do anything. The most wicked pains run through his body rising and falling in opposition to waves of sickness and fear. The day passes in delirium, and it is only when a jet of burning sick threatens to rebel up his gullet that he finally shakes himself free of his bedding. Too shaky to run or find a receptacle, he swallows it. Yuk. He can smell his fingers. Groaning, he doubles over, dropping his head between his legs. Squish. Something soft and delicious pillows him. He stays like that until he gathers strength enough to suppress his stomach, then stumbles to the sink for a glass of water, which he downs. Right.

In a guilty haze, he tries to tidy up. Sort it out. He moves dirty plates towards the kitchen, then brushes his hair. He collects clothes from the floor and puts them all in the washing machine. Switching it on, he hears the jingle of money from inside. Annoying. He tries to have a cup of tea but the milk is bad, and two drags on a joint left in the ashtray finishes him off. Back to bed. Crawling in from the wrong end, he leaves his head where his feet should be and shoves his ankles into the cold dead world under pillows.

His first sleep had been dead but the second is fraught with druggy dreams. Sweaty strangers in service stations whisper to dauntless old friends who take him to a lesbian bar where there's his mum. One corrupt beat loops constantly driving him onwards and onwards to Sydney, Addis, Rio, Hell, alongside a motorway. He is walking. He has lost everyone. He is relieved. On his map, all the countries in the world float away from Asia. No one had ever seen anything like it, the black smears left on the ocean. Further along, the motorway lifts into a flyover. He stays on the ground and is surprised to find a swimming pool begin in place of the road. It is the first of a string of pools that stretch across the country. This one is a West Coast design with slick, tiled edges and underwater lights that make it gleam and exaggerate the surrounding darkness. This must be it. As he walks on, it gets wilder, strong clumps of reeds break through the ceramic and line the pool edge, now a lake. He kicks at a busted tile, which falls into the water with a plop loud enough to drown out the overhead cars.

Soon, he sees it must be the ocean, and as far out as he can see, there is someone. Of course! A tiny, shiny bottom bobs above the waves then two legs wave above the horizon, then disappear as she dives down. He jumps in, swimming for miles blind underwater. The song is gone. Finally. Instead he can hear her laughter, like bubbles through the currents and then can see her, just a smudge of darkness in the black. The water is cold, but when his hand touches her stomach, it isn't. His arms pull her up close. He slips inside of her. Then he is awake, the sheets are wet, and the duvet cover is wrapped around his head. His body in seizures, he wrestles it free so he can see. The room might be burning, but she is too marvellous for him to tear his eyes away.

Palm to palm,
chest to chest,
mouth to mouth,
flesh on flesh.

WANK

FANTASIES HAVE FEELINGS TOO

Music ... *being* ... *the most beautiful* ... *of the art forms,* ... *is also* ... *the most* ... *corruptible.*

Song for Whoever

It is the 1970s. Everything is brown. In a chalet in the peaks of the Alps, live the Bricks. A father and a son, Kram and Stefan. Theirs is a close relationship, due primarily to the secluded nature of their living and secondarily to the fact that Stefan killed his offspring's mother. This is known. A secret shared between the two men, though not one that disturbs Kram. Kram is devoted to his father; they* are allies. To his childish recall, the murder (which is what it was) appeared clownish and absurd. It would be too far to go to say that Kram laughed about it. It was more, just, that it seemed okay. It never occurred to Kram, in the same way as it does not occur to any small child, that he, or at least his life, was different from other people's. A fact both secured and cemented by Kram not going to school. Stefan teaches his child himself, forgoing the rudimentaries of history or geometry or French, unless an aspect (and there are several) relates directly to music. Music is the only thing Kram is actively instructed in. His life a bizarre drill, where he is woken from sleep at any hour of the night and dragged to the piano, where he will be forced to play - first the pop songs ♪ of yesteryear, nursery rhymes ♩ and the like, but quickly progressing to more accomplished pieces ♫.

      During the day, there is music all the time. New releases from John Lennon and John Cage. These are always switched off for any birdsong. In the evenings, Kram reads music, disallowed from sitting at an instrument, he must visualise the sound in his head.

———————————

♪ Dear   ,
There comes a time in life when you have to hold yourself to account. Instead of assuming things are imposed on you by the world, try to examine what it is about you that attracts certain types of people and situations to you. Examine your own reactions, not only to things that upset you, but also to things that make you happy. Prolonged childhood is not such a bad state to exist in - it means that if and when you act responsibly, it gives you an enormous feeling of well-being and pride, disregarding that most of the world behave like this consistently. To not take responsibility for yourself means to impose the cost of your existence on the shoulders of the people who love you, which is unfair.

♩ Dear   ,
I am 29 years old and I know what the deal is OKAY!!!

♫ Dear   ,
I just don't want to see you get hurt anymore (mentally). I mean, this is crazy. You have a black eye!!!!

"That's how the great ones did it. What? You think Wagner had an orchestra on him at all times?"

His father is hard on Kram, so it is with some surprise when Stefan one day announces that he has been entered into a competition, and it is even more of a surprise when, in comparison to the other under-16s, Kram is very good. The best in fact. He wins. After the recital - a grand event taking over a rotting old chalet hotel across the Swiss border - Stefan and Kram are approached to take part in a panel debating how best to approach genius when it occurs in infancy. Mr Brick presents Kram as his subject, and his opinions are complimented by those of one D. L. Murray: *Methodical musical training implants knowledge in a different format to things which are simply taught. At onset of dementia, musical memory appears to be retained in much the same way muscle memory is. While a patient can have no idea of his own name, or that of the instrument before him, as well as no memory of ever having played it, if his fingers are guided to the correct starting point, he is as competent a player as before.*

Kram's life changes from one of seclusion between earth and sky. The Bricks plummet into civilisation. Plush airport lounges and underground trains. By the time he is nine years old,

Kram has appeared before audiences in Lisbon and Madrid, Tokyo and St. Petersburg, Dresden, Paris and Seville, Palma, Kyoto, Beirut and L.A., San Francisco, Marrakech, Belfast and Berlin. No longer failing resorts revamped as recital rooms, but extravaganzas legitimately occupying serious concert halls. Europe's Best Young Musician. Pomp, pushy parents and paraphrenia. Kram is a star. He has 'poise', is 'ethereal', his status exaggerated by the protective watch Stefan keeps over Kram. The child is never alone, and when addressed, turns silently to his father for a response.

A publisher approaches Stefan. A book. Stefan likes the idea. He has a decade's worth of notes charting Kram's progress: from comprehensive lists of physical ailments to flowery anecdotes of sleepwalking incidents (where Kram frequently appears to have forgotten everything he had been taught). *It seems that under times of duress, more complex arrangements are forgotten. Also noted in concentration camp survivors.* The book is compiled quickly and in no more than three months, a complete manuscript is in the publisher's hands. Its release generates a promotional tour, radio shows and discussion panels. In academic circles much is made of the title, bringing the book (which otherwise would surely have languished on the shelves of select specialist stores) to the attention of the greater general public. School run-mums fuel a frenzy of 'concern' about the detached way Kram is referred to. Letters are written and magazine articles published condemning it. The backlash extends to the circuit: Kram loses a competition.

Kram had always been a quiet child. Even when his mother was alive. One of those silent babies, whose pulse had to be checked before the snot was sucked out of his nose. He did not cry, nor did he attempt to imitate the boozy coos his mother bestowed upon him.

"Just like me. Right down to his fingertips." When he did speak, it was a complete sentence.

"There's a ladder over there."

It was the same with walking. No laboured crawl nor bottom shuffle. Aged one year and six months, he just got up and walked. Then proceeded to walk around the house all day, arms in the air, cheering at himself.

"Yeah, yeah, yeah."

It could be argued then, that it was less Mr

Brick's method of instruction, and more Kram's competent nature that made him what he was now largely accepted to be. A genius. Someone who at a very young age had surpassed what most people do with their 10,000 hours.

Kram could see how the world saw him. His youth. His potential. *Although he has not yet hit puberty, already signs of insubordination are showing.* One day Kram wakes up to find he hates his father.

"You play something," he yells. "You won't because you can't."

Kram is bored. That's what it is. Mr Brick understands. He thinks back to his own adolescence, which also arrived early. He shivers as he remembers how it lasted so long. He had married Kram's mother. He had thought he had been able to see his life so clearly, was disgusted by his upbringing and imposed characteristics, and was determined to redefine himself. Only once it was over and he found himself grown, the adult Mr Brick bore more similarities to himself aged 5 than himself aged 15. Stefan relents.

"You won't practise anymore. From now on, we are concerned only with the new. We are done with these 12 note octaves. Charmless modulations."

There follows a brief phase where Stefan

and Kram get on better than ever before. Left to his own devices, Kram decides to extend the neck on one of his violin, and adds three strings. The sound it makes is horrible, but it makes the birds sing. It is as if it is conducting them, torturing weird masterpieces out of the little critters.

Until now, Kram's playing had never been recorded, nor broadcast. (This is something his father is firm about - a fear of recorded music left over from a bad acid trip in 1968, where *Baby Love* had played four times during the course of a party. Stefan watched girls dance, laughing and dropping sexy wiggles and shimmies, and he thought of how many times those mass-produced grooves had been played, making the same sounds on record players everywhere, and how many sexy wiggles and shimmies had been dropped to the same beat. It made him feel sick. And he thought how this record would be played forever, the same. And it made him feel tired. The dancers seemed spoilt, and ignorant to the plea from the Queen of the Bunny Boilers. Loneliness has got the best of me my love.) However, this new territory seems too vital not to document. (Mainly because, for the first time, Mr Brick does not understand it). Words are not enough. *Writing about music is like dancing about architecture.* Kram likes that. Mr Brick sets up a compact cassette recorder and allows Kram to continue to experiment as he pleases, as long as the button is pressed.

For years, nothing is heard of the Bricks. Of course there is speculation in the press, and the occasional insight from the few friends Mr Brick keeps. A constant stream of invitations for Kram to appear at various events arrive, but are ignored. The second book to be released with the set of recordings, an instrument modification manual. Mr Brick also begins a portrait of his son.

On the book's completion he sends the manuscript with a note to his publisher. Two weeks later, he receives an excited acceptance, alongside assorted newspaper cuttings, mostly reviews but among them one news story about how in four provinces in north eastern China, Mr Brick's book had not been received as a case study, but as a Tao. There were some 500 inductees of the Brick Method, but even more astonishing, when you brought any number of Brick Method kids together, they* could perform identikit renditions of anything, note for note perfect, in time with each other, first go.

"Extraordinary," says Mr Brick.

He turns to the accompanying letter, so

smarmy it makes even slimy Mr. Brick squirm. Skip to the end. The last paragraph writes of an invitation from The Cincinnati Second Floor Orchestra – a group of free-thinkers and experimentalists who find Mr Brick's hardline efforts in keeping with their agenda. It could be what in modern terms one could call Kram's comeback. Mr Brick is pleased at the timing of the whole thing. From the front of the house, Mr Brick can hear his son whistling. What is that tune? Simple, silly - the song of clowns and serial killers alike. Gripped by a sudden paranoia, (denoting a disorder which has been argued in and out of existence, and whose every aspect is controversial), Mr Brick runs to the next room. The door is open, sunshine flooding the corridor. Damn your eyes. Looking down, Mr Brick sees that Kram has dismantled the piano. Not simply removing the soundboard to tinker with the tuning, he has untwisted every screw, unplucked every string. The tape recorder whirrs in the corner - he has recorded every second. Mr Brick starts to laugh.

"Genius!" he yells. "Genius!"

But there is something the matter. Kram has stopped whistling now.

"Rules relative to the behaviour of combatants." Kram is talking like a robot. Sounding like he used to when he was a kid, on the verge of hyperactivity. Annoying. "The belligerents enjoy no unlimited right regarding the choice of means to harm the enemy."

Then there is a drip. Then the whirring of the tape machine, then another. Mr Brick is so focussed on the sound that when it happens a third time, it sounds like it happens in reverse. Something being sucked up. Mr Brick's eyes adjust to the light so he can see there is blood daubed over the piano, crimson makes white keys look waxy, but sits heavy on the wood. Kram squats down beside where his father is (apparently) lying and holds out both hands, all eight fingertips missing. The kid tries to whistle, but his lips are too dry.

When the recording is released seven years later, alongside Mr Brick's 2nd volume, *The Entertainer*, D. L. Murray provides the sell: *The Final Brick Recording secures father and son a place in history, as unconscious prophets of the crash of civilization. Their cold-blooded analyses lays bare, with a gesture, a wink, the entire human beast. I wonder what outburst of indignation would greet a work by one of us naturalist novelists if we carried our satire of man in conflict with his passions to such an extreme. We certainly do not go so far in our cold-blooded analyses, yet even now we are often violently attacked. Obviously truth may be shown but not spoken. Let us, therefore, all make pantomimes.*

London, 1996

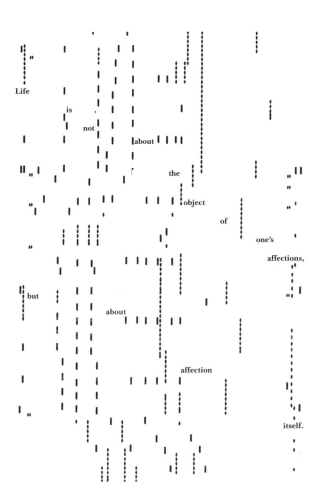

Life is not about the object of one's affections, but about affection itself.

WHO ARE YA?
(A world without)

The day Steve Jobs died, everyone went mental. *Here lies the last American that actually had a clue what he was doing!* Obama said. And the papers. People updated their facebooks. *1 man dies, 1000s cry. 1000s die, no one cries*, with pictures of starving Africans. I clicked the link. My computer froze. Third time that day. I tried force quit. No joy. I hold down the button until the screen goes blank. Then I press it again. Nothing. Again. Nothing. Again. A click sounds inside but nothing.

Fuck.

Fuck fuck fuck fuck.

I stroke the machine.

"Come on baby."

I could always fix my hi-fi like that when I was a teenager. I even sort of believed that electronic circuits responded to things like love. My friend's crazy Jamaican mum had had a thing with electronics. Most of the time it was fine, but when she got angry, or excited, her house would go haywire. The video machine would start rewinding or the microwave start up spontaneously, then thud, a small implosion and the thing would be dead. Watching telly, she would spit a running commentary to whatever was on, retelling events that had happened moments before to whoever was watching with her, as if divulging an illicit meeting that only she had been privy to.

"Ach, Janine, ya wikid chile, wikid wikid gal. She tro a single madda outa her home. Down out in the streets. Lord. It like your movin in the wrong line."

She would get het up, then the thing would blow.

"Ah ya kno it's for the bess. Mi an ole lady, mi don wanta be stuck to some tellyscreen. Mi should be out seen the worl."

I try again.

Nothing.

I notice a strange film covering the USB sockets. Like mildew, or a spider's web. I wipe it away.

Ok. Calm. Breathe.

I'd saved everything anyway and the hard drive was probably ok.

Still, shit.

I call my mum.

"Can't talk now! Can't talk now!" she yells down the phone, hysterical. She stays on the line for five minutes, screaming at me because her laptop had just given out as well. "I *will* help you. It'll *be* something simple. I just need to get these invites out this afternoon and be at the fair at four and..."

Right.

Weird though.

"Call Apple. Make an appointment."

And so I call the Apple shop.

"You are currently 400,000th in the queue."

Fuck that.

I hang up,

I try my computer again,

Still nothing,

Probably for the best. I'd spent days, if not months, and so years stuck to that machine. Even while the most beautiful sunsets unfolded outside my window, I would only glance away from it for a second. A few months before, I had had a wild bout of insomnia, not sleeping until 7am, and then only for a couple of hours. I tried watching TV, balancing my laptop on my chest and nestling under the covers. It was warm like a hot water bottle, which should make me sleepy, plus when I was a kid, as soon as the TV came on, I would pass out. It was something about the flickering light. On, off, on, off. It wasn't so much that it was reassuring, more that it was tiring to absorb. Not like the light from a computer. Constant white that zones you in, instead of out. Everything else disappears.

And where do you go on this machine, that can, at least academically, take you anywhere? Facefuck, soulsuck, tumblr.com. It feels like you're busy doing something, until you stop. Then you can't remember what you were doing, nor what you were supposed to be, and can't for the life of you figure out...

I spend the morning tidying the flat, listening to the radio.

The impact of a series of eruptions on the sun began arriving at Earth on Friday and could affect some communications for a day or so. Solar flares send out bursts of electromagnetic energy that strike the Earth's magnetic field. The most common impacts for the average person are the glowing auroras around the north and south poles, researchers said those could be visible this weekend. The magnetic blasts, likened to a tsunami in space, can also affect electronic communications and electrical systems.

I spend the afternoon scribbling down conspiracy theories about cyberconnectivity, which turns into a short story about Steve Jobs where his body is snatched by a fervent employee, driven out to the Joshua Tree, covered in meth and set fire to. Like Gram.

When it gets dark, I surprise myself by doing something I never do and call my mates.

"Long time."

"Pub?"

Outside is misty. Winter setting in. The streets are abandoned and seem eerie, but then they* always do when you've stayed in on your own for too long. Still, almost everywhere is shut and it's only 5 o'clock. Three different car alarms are going off. I jump on the 8. Upstairs, there is a girl bashing her iPhone against one of the railings to hold on to.

"Fucking bullshit thing."

I sit at the back of the bus, leaning my head against the window. When it stops at a traffic light, the juddering makes my forehead bash against it. Ow. I sit up straight and look into a first floor office. Some sort of media node. They are Apple'd up to the iBalls. A group of T4 presenter types are shouting at each other. Cos you can't hear what they are saying, it's funny. I laugh, and someone looks back at me. The bus moves. *The next stop is Bethnal Green station.* I swing up the aisle from pole to pole, then twirl onto the staircase and float down the stairs.

Out in the street I notice that almost all the screens in estate agents windows, usually showing house porn 24 hours, are blank.

There is a boy at the bus stop taking out his earphones and looking more closely at his iPod. Just then a Whitechapel posse bowl by. One grabs the thing out of his hands.

"Oi," his protest dies on the air.

"Stop chattin that shit brer."

"Yo, giv it t'me."

"Llow that, man."

"T's shi anyway."

"Fucking broke."

"Fuckin bust blud."

"Bare rinsed, ha ha ha."

"Oi. You. Pussyole. What you carryin round a busted mpfree player for anyway? Diiickhead."

They throw the iPod back at the kid. It lands on the pavement and smashes open, but he goes to pick it up with a dutiful air all the same. The boys walk towards me. When we are almost face to face, my knees buckle. *Shit.* I don't fall, but still.

"Ha ha ha, I think the lady likes you brer."

"Wot you sayin, wot you sayin."

Love you.

The Bahola is the best pub round East. Mainly because the normals don't go near it, and lesserly because they serve up free roast potatoes and white pudding every couple of hours.

"Stops this lot getting too smashed," the landlady nods to the shambolic line-up at the bar. "We call em Death Row. Ha, ha, ha. Alright Simon?"

Lily and Soph and Daps and his new bird.

"So I got a new computer today," Lily says.

The landlady lines up perfect Guinnesses in front of us.

"Mine fucking died."

We sit down with our pints at a table near the back, underneath the TV.

"Shit. You got it backed up?"

It smells like pissy swimming pools.

"Kinda."

"Yeah, except when I got it home," Lily is annoyed at being talked over, "it won't even switch on! It worked fine in the shop. They went through everything with me."

"What was it like?"

"What do you mean?"

"The Apple shop. Were they all like bummed out maaan?"

"Mourning Steve Jobs."

"Oh, yeah. Shit. I forgot. Ha. No. There was a weird vibe though. Lots of the tills weren't working, and there was a proper argument going on upstairs. This Russian dude, screaming down the place. But I mean, two fucking grand man. Pisstake."

"Yeah, but they'll sort it out. Apple are good like that you know. They care."

"Bullshit."

The landlady flicks on the TV above our heads.

"Football."

Death Row turns its gaze towards us.

Sky Sports is still on the build-up.

After initial technical difficulties...

She flicks to Fox News.

News of Jobs's death prompted reaction from all around the world. However, it seems that this great innovator of our time had not yet played his last hand. Reports first came in this morning of how Apple computer systems used at the White House had shut down. More reports followed from around the world, where it seemed that both business and personal customers were experiencing problems.

"Weird."

"Right."

Walter Isaacson, Jobs's biographer, says there may be a clue in his book (published by Random House) which hits the shelves tomorrow afternoon. Based on more than forty interviews with Jobs conducted over two years—as well as interviews with more than a hundred family members, friends, adversaries, competitors, and colleagues—Walter Isaacson has written a riveting story of the roller-coaster life and searingly intense personality of a creative entrepreneur whose passion for perfection and ferocious drive revolutionised six industries: personal computers, animated movies, music, phones, tablet computing, and digital publishing. The first recollections are of Jobs before he started Apple, during the time he was experimenting with psychedelics. It seems Jobs talked freely of his ideas concerning consciousness, and questioning as to whether an ideal machine could have a soul.

"He talked about Apple, said it was going to change the world."

Interestingly, one source says Jobs made claims that he would install hardware into every Apple *product, that will initiate a self-destruct mechanism upon his death. In his final interview, Jobs prophesied his death as heralding the start of "a second dark age, an anti-intellectual grey zone, where you will mass retreat into stupidity and superstition."*

It was thought that this was the sign of a great mind unravelling under pressure and there was at first talk about excluding it from the book out of respect to Jobs. Walter Isaacson-

"Although Jobs cooperated with this book, he asked for no control over what was written nor even the right to read it before it was published. He put nothing off-limits, and it was decided that the piece be included."

Despite worst fears still being unconfounded, it appears that the loss of Steve Jobs has left a very real vacuum in an increasingly virtual world. It seems that in death, as in life, Jobs knows exactly how to press our all our buttons...

The landlady flicks the channel back to Sky Sports. It's seconds before kick off. Some retarded-looking children are being escorted back into the tunnel as the camera sweeps the crowd, zooming in on fat drunk men whose faces are discoloured, claret and blue.

Thugs, yobs, hooligans and deadbeats, none of whom look like they have the slightest interest in changing the world, for better or for worse. They are pissed and hyperactive. They clamber up onto the flip-up chairs in the stands, leaning on each other's shoulders and raising arms in the air as they sway, shouting at the top of their lungs,

WHO A
WHO A
WHO A
WHO A
WHO A
WHO A

RE YA?
RE YA?
RE YA?
RE YA?
RE YA?
RE YA?

No. 9
No. 9   No. 9
No. 9   No. 9
No. 9   No. 9
No. 9   No. 9
No. 9
No. 9
No. 9
No. 9

NOTES ON THEY

° Everyone has a plan 'till they get punched in the mouth. *Interview: Boxing Biannual*, **Mike Tyson**

° they keep up a pretence; their respectability, their philosophy, their realism, are all attempts to gloss over, to make look civilised and rational something that is savage, unorganised, irrational. *The Outsider*, **Colin Wilson**

°they (pronoun), as subject of a verb 1 the people or things in question 2 people in general 3 people in authority. **OED**

° Good and bad men are less than they seem. *Specimens of the table talk of the late Samuel Coleridge*

° they'll never throw it back to you. [oasis]

°they turned away from him and again all became quiet. *The 7 That Were Hanged*, **Leonid Andreyev**

° As slick as you think you are. *That Day Will Come*, **Capleton**

°They walk along with us, that is for sure, and yet see where their heads are: in that fog compounded of neon, gin and peppermint emanating from the red and green shop sign above them. *The Outsider*, **Albert Camus**

° It was then that Titus roused himself and lifted his face from his arms and saw nothing but the flush of the dawn sky above him and the profuse scattering of stars. What were we <u>they</u>? *Gormenghast*, **Mervyn Peake**

° In any prison the warders in the punishment block are pure sadists, who volunteer for the punishment block solely because they delight in being able to kick any man senseless and get paid for it. *Who Guards the Guards?* **Brian Stratton**

°I explained that we were moving in. If they did not like it, they could go; if, on the other hand, they preferred to stay and share equally what was there, they were free to do so. They were not pleased. *The Day of the Triffids*, **John Wyndham**

°Consequently they suffer from the notion that everybody is assessing their progress and perhaps commenting on the absence of major works which would justify a certain amount of arrogance, or at any rate indigence and idleness. *dead as doornails*, **Anthony Cronin**

°They have all one breath; so that a man hath no preeminence: for all is vanity *Ecclesiastes 3: 19*

°And so the men from the caravans found them, the Fat Man and the girl in black with a baby in her arms, racing round and round on their mechanical steeds to the ever-increasing music of the organ. *After the Fair*, **Dylan Thomas**

°surrounded by the cool kids, that knew we were lame *this is a love song*, **Tony O'Neill**

° RAT: No, no. They're policemen *The Wind in the Willows*, **Kenneth Grahame**

°They deal with common everyday matters - the products we buy and discard, the places we leave behind, the corporations we inhabit, the people who pass at an ever faster clip through our lives. *Future Shock*, **Alvin Toffler**

°even though they see beached skulls. *Siren Song*, **Margaret Atwood**

°they knew that soon, even before they had gone to sleep, there would be a battle. *Only This*, **Roald Dahl**

°They would have to do something. *The Iron Man*, **Ted Hughes**

°After they croak, their circle of close friends explodes. *Rant*, **Chuck Palahnuik**

°They had been following him with their eyes, and when he glanced back at them, they burst out laughing. **Sylvia Plath**

°they clattered along the pavement and pushed folded newspapers into letterboxes, each bearing crossword puzzles, sports news and forecasts, and interesting scandal that would be struggled through with a curious and salacious indolence over plates of bacon and tomatoes and mugs of strong sweet tea. *Saturday Night & Sunday Morning*, **Alan Sillitoe**

°they've been cramped for too many years dancin in tight circles in depressin dingy little discos with no space and a strict 'dance like a square or you're out' policy. *Freaky Dancin*, **BEZ**

° First they ignore you. Then they ridicule you. And then they attack you and want to burn you. And then they build monuments to you. And that, is what is going to happen. **Nicholas Klein**

°they sat like automatons, one on each side of the fire. *Wuthering Heights*, **Emily Brontë**

°Paranoia saves lives. **BT**

°They must have dug and dug for hundreds of years. *Stig of the Dump*, **Clive King**

° No question of writing to Wild Children. They think in images--prose is for them a code not yet fully digested & ossified, just as for us never fully trusted. *T.A.Z.* **Hakim Bey**

°They are the Virtues, the Graces, the Beauties of the hurried mangled craziness of Monterey and the cosmic Monterey where men in fear and hunger destroy their stomachs in the fight to secure certain food, where men hungering for love destroy everything lovable about them. *Cannery Row*, **Steinbeck**

° it is easy to be paranoid in a Police state like this, that is my excuse anyway. **Nick Waplington**

°You always go on about this They. **JRTC**

°Crooks asked visitors their business so it could be discerned as to whether they were friend or foe. The latter always being those with a bill to be paid. *The Destinies of Darcy Dancer, Gentlemen*, **J.P. Donleavy**

°They styled themselves as active nihilists and I took pleasure in undermining their desire to live passionately. **Stewart Home**

° They say you're in cocaine, they say you should change your name, they even say your insane. **Bob Andy**

°There is no such thing as the State. And no one exists alone; 1st September 1939, **W. H. Auden**

° Deviance is not a quality of the act a person commits, but rather a consequence of the application by others of rules and sanctions to an 'offender'. **Becker**

°They watched me - old guys welded in wheelchairs for years, with catheters down their legs like vines rooting them for the rest of their lives right where they are, they watched me and knew instinctively that I was going. *One Flew Over the Cuckoo's Nest*, **Ken Kesey**

°I lived free, grubbing outside in the mud till I was black as a badger. **Laurie Lee**

°They looked vacantly after some figures in the crowd, and sometimes made a critical remark. *Two Gallants*, **James Joyce**

°You were an innocent child, it's true, but it's even more true that you've been a devilish human being!- **Franz Kafka**

°The beating of his heart, the sound of his breath, the blinking of his eyes - Blue is now aware of these tiny events, and try as he might to ignore them, they persist in his mind like a nonsensical phrase repeated over and over again. **Paul Auster**

° "They" also know that active opposition to their system is spreading. *The International Times Communique*, **The Angry Brigade**

°Poor men, think I, need not go up, so much as rich men should come down. **W.H.Davies**